A Note from the Author

The idea for *British Front* came to me when I saw a poster about racism in a window at Leeds University. The poster was the British flag, the Union Jack. But the red cross in the middle had been cut up and put back together in a different way, so that it looked like a swastika, the emblem the Nazis used in the Second World War.

The poster made me think about what Britain might be like one day in the future *if* racists got what they wanted.

In my story, Al and Jenny find themselves in a Britain of the future, in 2055. This Britain is the same as today except for one very big difference. Al and Jenny are enjoying life, and they're in love. Suddenly, they're in a new, nightmare country ... where they are not allowed to love each other.

Could this happen in Britain one day? Well, it's up to you to make sure that it doesn't.

For Freya,
with love

British Front

by

Eric Brown

First published in 2005 in Great Britain by
Barrington Stoke Ltd, Sandeman House, Trunk's Close,
55 High Street, Edinburgh EH1 1SR

ISBN 1-842992-94-5

Printed in Great Britain by Bell & Bain Ltd

Contents

Chapter 1

Leaving

My story is amazing – but it really happened. You can call me a liar if you like, but every word is true.

It began on that Saturday in 2005 when Jenny called for me. She was wearing tight jeans and a short T-shirt which showed her suntan and her hips.

"It's a great day for the trip, Al!" she said.

I pushed my bike along the front path. We were taking Jenny's tent and camping out on Branston Moor. *A night alone with Jenny*, I thought.

Mum was hanging out some washing in the garden. "And where are you off to?" she asked.

"I told you last night, Mum," I said with a sigh. "I'm off camping."

"With *her*?" Mum didn't like Jenny. She didn't like the clothes she wore, or the fact that sometimes Jenny wore make-up. "If you must go, I want you back first thing tomorrow morning."

"OK, Mum," I said. I looked over at Jenny. She was pretending she hadn't heard a thing. She had her back to us.

We got onto our bikes and rode off. I looked back at the house and waved.

Mum was standing in the garden and watching me go.

She looked small and lonely.

She didn't wave back.

My dad had died last year, and I missed him a lot. And Mum missed him too. Sometimes I found her crying softly to herself, with Dad's picture in her hand.

I felt bad that I was leaving her by herself, but I wanted to go camping with Jenny more than anything else.

We cycled out of the city. Jenny led the way up a steep hill and onto the moors at the top. They stretched out all around us.

"Your mum doesn't like me, does she?" Jenny said.

"I don't know ..." I said softly.

Jenny looked across at me. "Does she think I'm a slut?"

"Jenny!" I said with a laugh. "Of course not."

"Bet she does. I've seen her looking at me. I bet she thinks I'm really slutty!"

"It's not that," I said. "It's just that Mum's very old-fashioned."

"Does she think I'll do bad things with her little boy?" Jenny said.

I grinned.

Me and Jenny had never had sex, but we'd snogged a lot. When I wasn't with Jenny, I thought about her all the time. When I was with her, I felt like I was walking on air.

I loved her because she was funny and kind and caring. OK, she smoked cigarettes and drank Diamond White and wore sexy clothes. But the real Jenny was gentle and always thinking about others.

We cycled fast along the moorland road. At one point Jenny slowed down and stopped.

4

The sun shone on her face and the wind blew her long fair hair. "Look!" she called out. She pointed the way we'd come. "Doesn't it look great!"

She was pointing at the city. From a long way off, it did look good – all shiny glass windows, and buildings the same colour as honey. You couldn't see the litter from here, the dirty streets and poor houses.

I turned and stared at the moors ahead of us, covered with purple heather. "I think this looks even better," I said.

We set off again, leaving the city behind us.

Five minutes later – that's when it happened.

What happened?

Well, it's hard to explain. I can't tell you *why* it happened. All I can tell you is that it did happen. It was weird and creepy. I don't think anything like that has ever happened to anyone before. This is the story of what happened to Jenny and me that day in 2005.

Chapter 2

Swastika!

Jenny saw it first.

"Look!" she called.

The air was shimmering. At first I thought there was a heat haze, which sometimes happens above tarmac roads on very hot days. But the shimmering air was in the shape of a big circle. It hung just above the road in front of us.

Before Jenny had time to brake and stop her bike, she shouted out and hit the shimmering air. I yelled out and followed her.

I felt a quick pain, and then a sickness that began in my stomach and rose into my throat. I thought I was going to throw up. A loud buzzing filled my ears and I lost control of my bike.

I crashed off the road and into the ditch beside the road.

Jenny jumped off her bike. She ran back to me and scrambled down into the ditch.

"Al! Are you OK?" She looked terrified. Her face was white.

I knelt in the damp heather and rubbed my arm. My bike was upside down in the ditch beside me. "I'm OK. I just banged my elbow. I'll be fine."

"I thought you'd killed yourself, Al!" Jenny hugged me, and when she pulled away I saw tears in her eyes.

"What happened?" I said.

Jenny climbed out of the ditch. Then she held out her hand and helped me up.

We stood side by side in the road and stared around us.

"My God, Al!"

Now, this is the hard part to believe. I know, because I didn't believe it.

The moorland had vanished. Tall trees were growing on both sides of the road – not the heather and grass that had been there before. And the road was different too. It was a lot wider, and the tarmac was fresh and black, as if the road had just been made.

We held onto each other. We were very scared. Jenny was shaking with fear and so was I. What had happened to the beautiful moorland?

"Listen," I said. I had heard something.

We stood very still and listened.

I heard it again.

It was a deep rumbling roar like a hundred big engines.

Then I saw the line of vehicles – cars, lorries and tanks. They were far away up the road, between the trees.

We stared at them. Our mouths dropped open.

It was a huge group of army vehicles moving together up the road. There were tanks and troop carriers and rocket launchers.

That's odd, I thought, *army vehicles in the Yorkshire countryside.* But there was something even odder.

British Army trucks and tanks are normally painted green. But these vehicles were black.

Black.

That made me even more scared.

The first big tank was coming slowly towards us.

"Quick!" Jenny cried. She grabbed her bike and pulled it off the road into the ditch.

We bent down in the ditch as the roar of the engines on the road above grew louder and louder.

The line of vehicles swept past us.

At one point I poked my head up over the edge of the ditch and stared. Two great rocket launchers roared past, then tanks and trucks. I saw soldiers sitting on top of the tanks. They were all wearing black uniforms. Then I saw the strange sign painted on the sides of the tanks and trucks. It looked like a swastika – the emblem the Nazis had used in the Second World War.

I stared at Jenny. She had seen it too.

It was the British flag – the Union Jack. But it had been changed. In the middle of the flag was a big black swastika.

"I don't understand, Al!" Jenny said softly.

I said, "I know what it is! They're those people who dress up and play at soldiers at weekends."

Jenny was staring at me. "Yeah? And how often do they have tons of tanks and bombs and stuff like that?"

And what about the way the countryside is all different, with new trees and no moorland? What about the swastika flag? What's going on? I asked myself.

Jenny held my arm tightly. "Where are we, Al?"

"Wish I knew," I whispered.

Above us on the road, the last truck rolled past. Slowly, the sound of the engines grew softer. I was about to climb out of the ditch when I heard the sound of another vehicle. I ducked down.

The engine noise grew loud, then cut out as the vehicle stopped.

I peered through the grass above the ditch. A Land Rover stood in the middle of the road. As I watched, six men jumped down from the back.

At first I thought it was something to do with the long line of army vehicles we had seen. But this Land Rover was green, not black, and the men weren't in uniforms.

We hid down in the ditch so that they couldn't see us.

"OK," a man shouted. "It opened around here. They can't be far away. Spread out and look for them along the road, then in the woods."

Jenny hissed, "They're looking for us!"

"What do we do?"

Jenny looked over the top of the ditch, then ducked back down. "They're about ten metres along the road, with their backs to us. If we grab our backpacks and creep into the woods, maybe we can find somewhere to hide."

"What about the bikes?"

"Leave them here. We can't take them."

I took my backpack off my bike. Jenny got her tent and backpack from her bike and peered into the woods.

"Come on – follow me!" she whispered.

We crawled up the side of the ditch, through the grass and into the trees. We went as fast as we could on our hands and knees. *Any moment*, I thought, *someone will spot us and shout.*

We scrambled through wet bushes and ferns for five minutes. In front of me, Jenny stopped and looked over her shoulder. "They won't be able to see us now."

We stood up and ran through the woods, dodging trees and jumping over fallen tree trunks.

We must have run for miles. About half an hour later, we stopped. I was worn out.

"What now?" I asked.

"Shall we find somewhere to set up the tent for the night? Then wait till morning to see what to do next?"

I nodded. We set up the tent behind a bush. No-one could see it.

Jenny unpacked her bag. "Shit," she said.

"What?"

"I don't believe it! I forgot the camping stove! We can't cook anything. How do you fancy cold baked beans and raw eggs?"

"Have you got any matches?"

She patted a pocket in her jeans. "No, but I've got a lighter."

"Cool," I said. "We'll find some dry wood and make a small fire."

She looked at me. "What if those guys are still looking for us? They'll see the smoke."

I thought about it. "OK, we'll wait an hour, and then light the fire."

Jenny nodded. "Let's find some wood."

We spent the next ten minutes picking up small branches and twigs for our fire.

I was about to go back to the tent when I saw a few pages from an old newspaper on the ground. *Nice one*, I thought. A newspaper was just what we needed to start a fire.

I picked it up and went quickly back to the tent.

Jenny was crouching on the ground, making a pile of twigs and branches. I helped her.

Jenny took the newspaper and was about to tear it up and stuff it under the twigs. She stopped. She was staring at the front page. Her face was very white.

"Jenny, what's wrong?"

"Oh, my God," she whispered. "Look."

She passed the newspaper to me.

"What?" I said.

"Look at the date," she said.

I read the top of the paper. The *Daily Front*, it said. Funny, I never knew there was a paper called the *Daily Front*.

Then I read the date.

Monday, 24th July, 2055

"2055?" I whispered. What was going on?

Chapter 3
A Hole in Time?

Jenny stared at me. "2055. That's 50 years from now!"

"It's a mistake," I said. "The paper made a mistake."

Jenny turned to another page and stared at the date. "Well, there's a mistake on this page, too. Look."

It was the same date.

Monday, 24th July, 2055

"It's a joke," I said. "It's a joke newspaper."

Jenny looked at me with big eyes. "Oh, yes? And were the army vehicles a joke, and the way the countryside looks all different now?"

I just shrugged. I felt sick.

Jenny said, "Did you hear what they said, those guys in the Land Rover?"

I shook my head. I couldn't think straight.

"They said, 'It opened around here. They can't be far away'." Jenny stared at me. "What opened, Al? Some kind of ... I don't know ... a hole in time? Is that it? Have we fallen through a hole in time?"

"No!" I shouted. "That can't happen!"

Jenny held the newspaper up in front of my eyes. "Then how do you explain this, Al?"

I grabbed the newspaper from her and read it. My head felt as if it was going to burst.

Jenny sat next to me and read the paper, too.

The headline said: *Troops Battle in Yorkshire!*

Jenny read out the report: "*British soldiers are still fighting the last of the terrorists in Yorkshire. The battle of Branston Wood began on Saturday. The UK Army said today that they are confident of victory ...*"

She shook her head. "So that explains the army," she said.

We sat still for a long time. We didn't say anything.

"Jenny," I said, at last.

"Mmm?"

"What can we do? I can't believe we're in the future. Do you know what that means?" I looked at Jenny, then went on, "Everything we know, everyone we know ... Everything has gone."

Jenny said, "My mum and dad. They'll be so old now, really ancient. God, Dad'll be 90, if he's still alive!"

"My mum, my uncles ..." I said. If she was still alive, my mum would be over 80.

We crawled into the tent and lay down. Jenny put her hand out and I pulled her towards me. For a long time, we just lay there in each other's arms.

It was getting dark outside when, all at once, Jenny sat up.

"What is it?" I asked.

"I thought I heard something!" She scrambled from the tent, pulling me after her.

We stood outside the tent and listened. I heard something. A man's voice. Then I heard the sound of a stick, banging at the ferns and grass. They were still looking for us!

Jenny grabbed her backpack. "Come on!"

We were about to start running when I heard a sound behind us. I turned.

A boy stepped through the trees and stopped. He looked a year or two older than us, perhaps 17 or 18. He stared at us. "Stop!" he said.

I froze. Jenny pulled my hand. My heart missed a beat. I looked around wildly. Were other people going to step from the shadows and all come round us? The boy was looking at me as if he'd never seen anyone like me before. He wore a shiny green tracksuit and his hair was cut very short.

I looked around. There must be a way to escape. But there were shadows all around us, and I was sure that other people were hiding there too ...

The boy said, "Don't run! I can explain!"

In panic I reached forward and punched the boy in the chest. He didn't expect that and he fell over backwards, crying out as his head hit a log.

We ran.

I have never run so fast in my life.

Hand in hand we raced through the woods, jumping over roots and bushes and logs. My heart pounded. I heard shouts behind us. Jenny dragged me left and right, trying to lose the people who were after us.

Who were they? What did they want? How did they know we were here?

My head was full of questions, and fear.

We ran through the trees for ages. The sky was dark now and there was a big moon high in the night sky.

At last we came to the edge of the woods. Only then did Jenny stop.

I took deep breaths, leaning against a tree. In the moonlight, I could see some open fields. Jenny pointed.

"Look, a farmhouse. There's a barn. Let's spend the night there."

We left the woods and ran across the fields towards the barn. When we reached the building, we stopped and looked back. Everything was still and silent. Moonlight fell on the trees, turning them silver. It looked beautiful. It was hard to believe that the woods were full of people, hunting for us.

We slipped into the barn and Jenny went up a ladder into a dark hayloft. I followed. She pulled a torch from her backpack. We made a bed from a pile of hay and snuggled down.

"Hungry?" Jenny asked.

"Have you got any food?"

She pulled out some crisps, a tin of baked beans and two Mars Bars.

"Is that all we've got?" I asked.

"Some raw eggs ..." Jenny laughed.

We lay side by side and ate the Mars Bars and crisps.

I said, "Jenny, we're all alone, now. We have nothing."

She put an arm around me. "How can we be alone when we have each other? Did I ever tell you how much I love you, Al?"

I smiled.

Jenny switched off the torch and kissed me.

Chapter 4
Life in the Future

I woke up early in the morning. The sun was shining through a hole in the roof. I sat up. At first I didn't know where I was. Then I remembered.

We were in the future, Jenny and me.

The future ... 2055.

When Jenny woke up, I said, "What now? We've only got a tin of beans and some raw eggs."

Jenny thought for a while. "We'll go into the city and buy more food there."

I stared at her. "What with? What if the shops won't take our old money?"

Jenny made a face. "Well, let's just hope they will ..."

We crept out of the barn and ran across the fields. We walked along beside the road, ready to leap behind a tree if a car passed.

One hour later we came round a bend in the road and stopped. There was the city, in the valley in front of us. But it was a very different city to the one we had left yesterday.

The buildings were taller, and many were made out of glass – like something in a *Star Wars* film. In between the new buildings, we could see older houses, like the ones Jenny and I had lived in. We walked into the city along a street with the sort of houses we knew on each side. In that street, it was almost hard to believe that we were in the future.

But the people were different. They wore odd clothes, all in bright, shiny colours. And they stared at us as we walked down the street.

Jenny whispered to me, "They're staring at us because of our clothes!"

I didn't say anything, but I knew she was wrong. They weren't staring at our clothes. They were staring at me.

I said, "Jenny, what's odd about these people?"

"Odd?" she said. "I don't know."

"They're all white," I said. "Where are all the Asians?"

"My God," Jenny said softly. "You're right!"

"I'm the only person with brown skin," I hissed. "That's why they're all staring at me."

In my own time, 2005, my city had all kinds of people: black and white and yellow, and every colour in between. Now, I could see only white faces. And they were all staring at me.

I stopped walking and gripped Jenny's hand. "I think this was a mistake," I said. "Come on, let's get back to the barn and think about what to do next."

Jenny nodded. We turned around. We didn't get far.

Someone was standing in front of us, staring down at us.

"What are *you* doing here?" the man asked, glaring at me.

Another man came up to us. "Yeah, get back to where you belong, darkie!"

More and more people came round us, shouting, calling me names. "Get back to Pakistan!"

"Leave him alone!" Jenny shouted.

"Shut your face, Paki-lover!" a woman spat. "Get back to Paki-land with him!"

I felt tears sting my eyes. I wanted to shout and hit out, but I knew that would be a mistake.

"We should hang you from the nearest lamppost!" a teenager cried. He pushed his ugly face close up to mine.

I had never thought that people could be full of so much hate. People had been racist in my time, of course. Some idiots had called me names, and made stupid remarks. But it had been nothing like this.

The people were getting at me because of the colour of my skin.

Soon there was a crowd around us, pushing Jenny and me, spitting at us. I wondered if soon someone might pull out a knife ...

31

Then I heard another shout. "What's going on here? OK, break it up! Move away! I said – *break it up*!"

Like magic, the crowd moved away. I stared at the tall figure who stood in front of us. He wore a black uniform and carried a huge gun in his right hand. A policeman? A soldier?

I smiled at the man. I felt good – for a second. Then I looked at the man's face. It was full of hate. He shook his head and said, "A Paki? Well, well, well." He stood up tall and said, "Under Emergency Law 347, I arrest you. I think you may be a terrorist and working against the State. Anything you say will be taken down and used in evidence ..."

Before I could say a word, he snapped a pair of handcuffs around my wrists. Then he did the same to Jenny and dragged us towards a black van parked at the side of the road.

Welcome to Britain, 2055!

Chapter 5

Prisoners!

We were taken to a police station.

I was pushed into a tiny cell. The door was made of bars. They dragged Jenny along the corridor. A door opened and closed with a bang. I heard Jenny shout out – then everything was still.

I sat on the floor, my back against the bars. A camera stared down at me from the ceiling.

I had never felt so lonely in all my life. I was scared. But the odd thing was that I was more scared for Jenny than for me.

And that was weird – because Jenny was the strong one. It was always Jenny who led the way, who decided what to do.

I just went along with what she said.

But now I was scared about what the police might do to her …

As I sat there, in the silent cell, I knew how much I really loved Jenny. *If anything happens to her*, I said to myself, *I don't want to go on living.*

I pressed my face to the bars and tried to look down the corridor. "Jenny!" I hissed.

"Al! Are you OK?" Jenny called out.

"I'm fine," I said. Then I laughed.

"What?" she said.

"Just think," I whispered. "Yesterday we set off to the moors with our tent … and today we're 50 years in the future."

"Yeah. In a police cell and they think we're terrorists."

She didn't say anything for a while, and then she went on, "What happened to the England we knew, Al? How did these people come to power?"

I thought about that. The old England hadn't been perfect. It was full of racists, people who hated anyone different. I thought about what people had called me in my own time ...

Black bastard!

Paki pig!

No, my England hadn't been perfect ... But it was better than this – the England of 2055.

I said, "Jenny, even in our time there were people like this. Racists. They wanted to get rid of everyone who was different to them."

"It looks like they got what they wanted," Jenny said.

"Shh! What's that?" I hissed.

A door opened and we heard boots marching along the corridor. Two policemen in black uniforms stared through the bars at me. They had small flags on their uniforms, the same as the flags I'd seen on the side of the vehicles yesterday – a Union Jack with the black swastika in the middle. The sight of that flag nearly made me sick.

One of the policemen pointed at me. "Stand up!"

Slowly I got to my feet.

He pressed a button on his belt and the bars slid apart. I moved back from him, into the cell. "What do you want?" I said.

"Just a few questions," the first policeman said.

They stepped into the cell and grabbed my arms. I tried to fight, but they were much stronger than me. They dragged me out of the cell and down the corridor. Behind me, I could hear Jenny shouting.

We came to a silver metal door and the first policeman touched the button on his belt again. The door opened and we marched inside.

A man sat behind a small table. He had a square face and short, silver hair. He stared at me. His face twisted, as if I were a bad smell.

The policemen pushed me into a chair, then clipped a belt around my chest so that I couldn't move.

The policemen left the room and the door banged shut behind them. There was no more noise. I stared at the desk in front of me.

"You can make this easy for yourself," the man behind the table said. "I'm going to ask you a few questions, and you will tell me the truth. If you don't say anything, or if you lie, then this is what you will feel."

He touched something under the desk. An electric jolt shot through me, coming from the belt that held me in the chair.

I yelled with pain. My face was wet with sweat.

"Now," the policeman said, with a smile, "what's your name?"

I answered, "Ali Iqbal Aziz."

"How old are you?"

"16."

He leaned forward. "How did you get into the country? Who brought you here?"

I shook my head. "I've always lived here. I was born in Bradford."

He touched something under the desk. Pain shot through me. I cried out.

"I said, 'How did you get into the country?'" the man went on.

I said, "I was born here. I'm English!"

The pain, again. It was as if a red-hot iron bar had been put on my chest. "No!" I cried.

The pain stopped suddenly. I sat slumped in the seat. I was sweating.

The policeman said, "You're lying, Aziz. There are no more of your people in England. The British Front made sure of that!"

"The British Front?" I whispered.

"We rule the country, now. We made sure we got rid of people like you."

I stared at him. The hatred in his eyes made me think about the people I'd seen in the street. Their eyes had looked at me in the same way.

I said, "You sent my people back to Pakistan?"

I will never forget what he said then.

He laughed. "We sent some of them back – those that wanted to go. The others ... well, we got rid of them in our own way."

I felt sick.

The policeman leaned forward. "Who is your contact in the terrorist group?"

I shook my head. "I don't know what you're talking about. I don't know any – *aggh*!"

Terrible pain ripped through me.

The policeman said, "Where are you staying in England? Your address?"

At least I could tell him that. "I live at number 46 Bradley Avenue with my mother, Rizwana. My dad, Mohammed, is dead. I have a sister, Zara, at university. I was born and bred in England. My best friend is Jenny Stewart, who isn't bothered about the colour of my skin! No—!" I cried, as pain shot through my body.

"Silence, liar!" the policeman snarled.

But I went on. "I was born in 1989, in an England where everyone was equal. I don't know how I found myself in this racist country!"

He stared at me. Something changed about the way he was looking at me.

Very softly he said, "You said you were born in 1989, and you don't know how you came here, to 2055?"

I nodded.

He said, "What's the last thing you remember about your own time?"

"We were cycling along the moor road. We saw something above the road in front of us. The air was shimmering. We passed though the haze – and then everything was different."

The policeman leaned back in his chair and stared at the ceiling. He was whispering to himself, "So it is true. The terrorists have developed a time-transfer system ..."

He stared at me. "Why do the terrorists want you and the girl?"

I shook my head. "They don't want us. It was an accident. We didn't want to come here."

He reached under the desk again, and I expected another jolt of pain. Instead, the door opened and the two policemen marched into the room.

"Take him back," he said.

The policemen took me out of the chair and dragged me from the room. I could hardly walk. The electric shocks had made me weak.

They marched me along the corridor and threw me into the cell.

I fell against the wall, shouting out in pain.

Jenny was yelling, "Al, what did they do to you?"

The policemen moved along the corridor. I heard them open a cell door.

"You, girl!" a policeman said. "Out!"

"No!" I cried.

"Let go of me!" Jenny yelled.

Seconds later I saw the two policemen struggling along the corridor. Jenny was fighting like a tiger, and I felt my heart leap with pride and fear.

"Jenny!" I shouted. I tried to stand up, but my legs were too weak.

The policemen and Jenny moved away and I sat against the wall and wept.

Chapter 6
No Way Back ...

Later, they came back with her.

She wasn't struggling and fighting now. They dragged her down the corridor and locked the cell door behind her.

When the policemen left, I pressed my face against the bars of my cell and hissed, "Jenny, are you OK?"

She was sobbing. "I'm fine. I'm not going to let them win!"

"They ... they tortured you, didn't they?"

She said, "But I didn't cry, Al. I wasn't going to let him see me cry!"

"What did he ask you?"

"He thought I was a terrorist. He wanted to know where the terrorists were hiding. I told him the truth. I told him that we came from the past. The weird thing was, he seemed to believe me."

"I know," I said. "I told him about the past, too. He said something about a time-transfer system. Then he asked why the terrorists wanted you and me."

Silence. At last Jenny said, "Perhaps they do, Al."

"What? The terrorists want us? But why?"

"I don't know ... But remember the Land Rover yesterday, Al? After all those army trucks had gone by, there were those men in a Land Rover. They stopped and started

46

looking for us. Maybe they were the terrorists."

"But what do they want with us?" I asked.

Jenny was silent again, and then she said, "I don't know, Al. I just don't know."

A long time passed.

Every time I heard a sound, I jumped. I thought it was the policemen, coming back to ask us more questions, to torture us again.

The lights in the cell and the corridor went out. Through a high, barred window I could see a patch of sky. It was getting dark.

We were about to spend our second night in the future.

Jenny called out to me, "Al? Are you still awake?"

"Mmm."

"Al, I miss ... everything. Home. My mum and dad. Friends. The real England."

"So do I," I said.

"It *was* a good place, wasn't it? Our England?"

I thought about that.

"I don't know about *good*," I said. "I mean, it was a better place than this. But it wasn't perfect. There was lots of racism ..."

Jenny said, "But not everybody was racist, were they? I mean, me and my mates ... my mum and dad."

I smiled to myself. "Of course everybody wasn't racist. But it only takes a few bad people to make life terrible for anyone who's different."

"But how did England get to be like this? How did it get so bad, so that *everyone* was racist?"

"The wrong people came to power," I said. "They spread their hate of black people. It was like Nazi Germany. Hitler made so many people hate the Jews that it got to be *normal* to hate Jewish people ..."

Jenny said, "At least there are the terrorists. They're fighting against the British Front." She didn't say anything for a long time. Then she whispered, "Do you think we'll ever get back to our own time?"

I said, "No, I don't think so, Jenny. I mean, how can we?"

Then I heard Jenny crying in the darkness, and there was nothing I could do or say to help her.

Chapter 7
Escape!

"Al! Wake up!" It was Jenny shouting at me.

"What?" I said. At first, I thought she was in the cell with me. Then I remembered that she was locked up along the corridor.

She was yelling. "Wake up!"

I sat up and stared into the darkness. "What is it?"

"I heard noises. Shouts. A gunshot."

I stood up and went over to the bars on my door. I heard the sounds of shouts and running feet. Then a bang. Another gunshot ...

"What's happening?" Jenny said.

I tried to look along the corridor, but it was too dark to see anything.

The lights in the corridor flashed on suddenly, and the door at the far end burst open.

A man and a woman ran along the corridor. They were dressed in brown combat trousers and brown shirts and had stockings over their heads.

The woman stopped outside my cell and shouted, "Stand back!"

I got back against the far wall of my cell.

The woman pointed something at the lock on the bars. The lock exploded. She kicked open the door and pulled me out of the cell. "Follow us! Do as we say! Fast!"

I ran out of the cell. Along the corridor, the man was pulling Jenny out of her cell. She ran to me and I hugged her.

"Come on!" the woman cried.

We ran down the corridor after the man and woman who had rescued us.

We ran through an office. Dead policemen lay on the floor. I have never seen so much blood.

"Along here!" the woman cried, and set off down another corridor.

We ran after the man and woman. I could still hear the crack of gunshots outside the building. We came to a door and the woman kicked it open, then stopped and peered outside.

We were at the back of the police station. The sound of gunfire was loud now. As we stood by the door an explosion and a huge crash threw us to the floor.

We picked ourselves up. Then the woman turned to us and said, "Listen carefully. Follow Mac, here. He'll take you somewhere safe. If you lose him, we'll meet you at dawn on the forest road, where you left your bicycles. Do you understand?"

Jenny nodded. I said, "Who are you? Why have you saved us?"

"We call ourselves freedom fighters," the woman said. "But we'll explain everything later."

She peered through the open door again, then tapped the man on the back. "It's clear. Go!"

The man, Mac, ran through the door and we followed him into the darkness. We sprinted across a car park and jumped over a low wall.

"Stop!" a voice cried.

I heard shots behind us. In front of us, Mac cried out and stopped suddenly, then slumped to the ground, groaning. I knelt beside him, reached out and felt the hot blood on the back of his shirt.

He rolled onto his back and said, "Go! The forest road! I said *go*!"

I grabbed Jenny. "Come on!"

Gunshots cracked behind us. I heard bullets hitting the walls around us.

I held Jenny's hand and we sprinted down a short street, then turned left along a main road. I dragged her down an alley and we ran for what seemed like hours, heading away from the city.

Behind us, we could hear the sound of the fighting still going on in the darkness – machine-gun fire and explosions and the wail of police sirens.

Hand in hand, we ran for our lives.

Chapter 8
The Graveyard

"Stop!" I said.

Jenny stared at me. "What?"

I pointed across the road. "Look. I know where we are. That's the Muslim graveyard where my dad is buried."

Jenny tugged my hand. "Come on. We need to keep going."

I looked at her. "Jenny, I want to see my dad's grave. It's important. I want to know that ... I want to know that at least something of the past is still here."

She bit her lip, then nodded. "OK," she said. "But we can't be long."

We crossed the road and walked through the gates of the graveyard.

In my own time, I had visited my dad's grave every week. It helped me think about him, all the good times we had had, before his heart attack.

Now I stopped and stared around at the moonlit graveyard.

"Jenny ..." I said in a small voice.

"What's wrong?"

I felt tears filling my eyes. "Look, they've ... they've taken away all the gravestones!"

I stared about at the old graveyard – except it wasn't a graveyard any more. It was a garden, planted with bushes and trees and flowers.

I ran to the corner where my dad's grave had been. I knelt down to look at his grave. His gravestone wasn't there. A rose bush grew instead.

I shouted out.

Jenny joined me and knelt down. I felt her arms around me. "Oh, Al, I'm so sorry."

I said, "Jenny, not only have they got rid of all my people – they've got rid of the dead, too! What kind of monsters are they?"

Jenny hugged me tight. "They're inhuman monsters," she said, very softly. "Or perhaps, even worse, they're *human* monsters."

We stood up and walked out of the garden. As we ran along the dark streets, I said, "Jenny, I don't think I can live in this time. I think I'd rather die."

"Don't say that!"

"It's true."

Jenny said, "Maybe we can join the freedom fighters. We can fight against the British Front."

Soon we'd left the city behind and 30 minutes later we were walking on the road that ran through the forest. Every time we heard a car, we dived into the ditch and hid.

Jenny looked up and down the road. "It was somewhere around here that we came through the hole in time," she said.

We looked along the ditch for our bikes.

"Here!" I cried. We scrambled into the ditch and I found my bike. It made me remember all the good times I'd had with Jenny in the past.

"Now," I said, "we sit here and wait."

We didn't have to wait for long.

In the east, the sky became lighter. Birdsong filled the air. I held Jenny to me and looked around for any sign of the freedom fighters.

Minutes later I heard a sound behind us. I turned round. A shape came from the woods and jumped down into the ditch.

I stared.

It was the boy I had punched in the woods.

He smiled. "It's good to see you again," he said.

"What do you want with us?" I asked. "Why did your people rescue us from the police station?"

The boy reached out and touched my shoulder. "We rescued you because we need your help," he said.

Jenny laughed. "How on earth can we help you?"

The boy went on to tell us. "The other day we opened a time-frame on the road. We were going to send one of our people back to your time, to tell your government what was happening here. But just as he was about to go, you cycled though the frame. It shattered and our man couldn't use it."

My head was spinning. I felt dizzy.

Jenny said, "I still don't see. How can we help you?"

I smiled. I thought *I* knew how we could help the freedom fighters.

The boy said, "We're going to open the time-frame again today. We'll send you back home. We want you to help us fight the evil of the British Front."

I hugged Jenny. We both felt so happy.

We were going back to our own time!

Chapter 9
Back from the Future

We crouched in the ditch and stared at the boy with the short hair and the green tracksuit.

"You can send us back?" Jenny said.

The boy nodded. "We'll give you information for your government. Names of people in the British Front. We'll give you newspapers to prove your story. If you tell the people in your government, perhaps they can stop this terrible future from happening."

"But will they believe us?" Jenny asked. "Wouldn't it be better if one of your own people were to go back and tell them about all this?"

The boy smiled. "We thought about sending one of our freedom fighters back. In the end, we thought that you would do a better job. You see, we'll send you back home, but it will be a year *after* you vanished."

Jenny shook her head. "But why?"

I said, "I think I understand."

The boy went on, "Think about it. We'll send you back to 2006, not 2005. That means you'll have been missing for a year. You'll turn up with information from the future and your incredible story. The TV and newspapers will be full of what happened to you. Your government will have to believe you!"

The boy took a small parcel from his backpack and passed it to Jenny. "In here there are newspapers and important lists, names and addresses," he said. "And there are also photographs of some of the dead people that the British Front killed."

Jenny slipped the parcel into her backpack.

I gripped her hand. "We're going home, Jenny. We're really going home!"

The boy looked sad. "I can only dream of what your time must be like."

I said, "You could come with us."

He smiled. "My home is here. I have work to do. We need to keep on fighting the British Front."

He pointed along the road. "The time-frame will open in three minutes. Get ready to ride through it!"

We pulled our bikes out of the ditch and climbed onto them. We waited, side by side, like cyclists at the start of a race.

The boy looked at his watch. "30 seconds to go," he said.

I felt excitement fizz inside me. My heart pounded. I looked at Jenny and smiled.

"15, 14, 13 ... Get ready!"

I looked back at the boy. "Thank you for everything," I said.

Then I heard the sound of an engine.

In the distance, I saw the shape of a huge black army truck speeding towards us. It would reach us in seconds.

"How long to go?" Jenny cried.

The boy looked at his watch. "9, 8, 7 ..."

Ahead, above the road, the air shimmered. *The time-frame*!

"Go!" the boy cried.

On the other side of the time-frame I could see the black army truck hurtling towards us.

I stepped on the pedals and raced forward on my bike, with Jenny at my side on hers. I felt the wind in my hair as we sped towards the time-frame. I shouted out in fear.

We were close to the shimmering air, but the army truck was getting closer and closer on the other side of it.

It felt as if we were heading straight for the vehicle. There was only the time-frame between us and the truck.

Seconds later, we hit the shimmering air. I felt a quick pain shoot through my body, and then a sickness rise from my stomach. I wobbled, lost control of my bike and fell off.

But something was different now. I couldn't hear the army truck any more.

I felt a hand on my arm, lifting me up. Jenny was staring at me and she was crying. Tears ran down her face. I hugged her to me and we looked around us.

The woods were gone. All around us lay the moors, right over to the horizon, shining in the morning sun.

I looked back at where the time-frame had stood, but, of course, it was no longer there.

"We're home," I said. "Did it really happen, or was it a dream?"

Jenny pulled the parcel out of her backpack. "This is all the proof we need," she said.

We climbed back onto our bikes and set off back towards the city.

On the way home, Jenny bought a newspaper. The date was the 29th of July 2006 – a year since the day we set off for Branston Moor.

We rode home. We stopped at the end of Jenny's street. "Al ..." she said softly, "our parents must think we're dead."

"Perhaps they think we were murdered," I whispered.

She smiled at me, sadly, as I kissed her and said goodbye.

I rode home through the city. I passed crowds of people. I felt tears in my eyes, and a lump in my throat.

You see, I was home. The people around me were black and white and brown and yellow. They were Christian and Muslim and Hindu and Jewish ...

I stopped my bike at the side of the road and looked around at all the people walking along the pavement. So many different faces.

Then I set off home. I felt like shouting. I was so glad to be back.

I jumped off my bike and walked up the front path. My heart was beating fast and I felt dizzy. Mum hadn't seen me for a year. I wondered how she'd be.

I knocked on the door.

A minute later I saw my mum's shape through the glass. She pulled open the door and stared at me. Her hair had gone grey since I last saw her, and she looked older and smaller.

"Ali?" she said. "Is it really you, Ali?"

And then she was hugging me and we were both crying. "A miracle!" she cried. "My son has come home at last!"

She stood back and looked at me. "But where have you been all this time?"

"It's a long story," I said. "But it's great to be back!"

Chapter 10

We Must Warn the World!

The next day I met Jenny in the Muslim graveyard. I got there first and went over to my dad's grave. I knelt down and looked around at the other gravestones. Around me, people came and went. They were putting flowers on the graves, kneeling and praying softly.

I wanted to tell them what had happened to me. I wanted to tell them that in 50 years the graveyard might be dug up, all the bodies and the gravestones taken away, destroyed.

But there's a chance the future might be different now.

Yesterday the police saw us and asked us about what had happened. They wanted to know where we'd been for one whole year. We told them, and Jenny gave them the parcel with all the information from the year 2055.

After that, last night, the phone didn't stop ringing. Newspapers and TV stations wanted to talk to us. When I got up this morning, reporters were knocking on the door. I looked through the front window and saw a TV van parked in the street and about 20 reporters in the garden.

So then I phoned Jenny to find out if we could meet up. I crept out of the back door and ran all the way to the graveyard.

Jenny arrived ten minutes after me. "Sorry I'm late, Al! You should've seen all the fuss in our street! There were reporters everywhere and people phoning all the time."

"Tell me about it!" I laughed.

"I sneaked out the back door, but a reporter saw me and chased after me. I had to run like hell before I got away."

She looked around at the graveyard. "Al, did it really happen? Did we really get transported to the future?"

We didn't say anything for a minute. We held hands and stared down at my dad's grave.

I said, "I've been thinking, Jenny. About what happened to us."

She looked at me. "And?"

I said, "It's made me stronger. Being with you, seeing how brave you were ... And something else. I'm stronger because I've seen what hatred really is like, and I got through it." I smiled. "I was always shy before, wasn't I? Always timid and I never said much. I'm stronger now."

After a time Jenny said in a small voice, "I'm not sure I can go through with it, Al."

I stared at her. "With what?"

"All the fuss. The TV and papers. They all want to talk to me. Someone from the government rang up. They want to see us later today."

I nodded. "They rang me, too. They're coming up to Bradford at three o'clock."

Jenny shook her head. "I didn't think it would be like this. We'll be famous. Won't we? We're like ... like a circus show. *The kids from the future!*"

I thought about what the headlines might be –

Back from the Future!

Missing Pair tell of Racist State!

Incredible Journey through Time!

I said, "But we've got to tell our story, Jenny. We've got to tell everyone what happened. If we don't ... Well, look at what happened in the year 2055. Just think about it. If we say nothing, then perhaps thousands of people will die. My people, Asian people and black people and anyone who isn't white ..."

Jenny nodded. "Just because of the colour of their skin," she said in a whisper.

"I want to live in a *free* country," I said.

Jenny looked at me and tears filled her eyes. "We've got to tell our story, Al, haven't we? It's the only hope."

I knelt beside my dad's grave and picked up a handful of soil.

I let it fall through my fingers. "I love this country," I said. "I don't want the racist future to happen."

"Perhaps it won't," Jenny said. She smiled at me, "Thanks to us."

I stood up and kissed Jenny, and then we left the graveyard hand in hand.

Later that day we faced the cameras and told the world what had happened to us.

And this is our story. I know it sounds incredible but it's true. Please believe me, because it happened, every last detail. Jenny and I saw the future, and we did not like what we saw.

But I believe we can change the future. I think of Jenny, and her love for me, and I think about how much I love her ... and I *know* there is hope.

Barrington Stoke would like to thank all its readers for commenting on the manuscript before publication and in particular:

Jodie Andrews
Jade Babet
Emily Baird
Anna Bradshaw
Steph Brown
Shona Burns
Ann-Carole Chamberlain
Nicole Dodd
Megan Doran
Clare Duncan
Adam Jensen
Charlotte Luke
Natalie Martin

Keith McKenzie
Rachael Rodgers
Mary Russell
Peter Sansom
Craig Sherwood
Tammy Smith
Elaine Timoney
Kerry Turnbull
Ann Tutt
Jessica Wells
Jacqueline Wilson
Martin Yeatman

Become a Consultant!

Would you like to give us feedback on our titles before they are published? Contact us at the address below – we'd love to hear from you!

Barrington Stoke, Sandeman House, Trunk's Close,
55 High Street, Edinburgh EH1 1SR
Tel: 0131 557 2020 Fax: 0131 557 6060
Email: info@barringtonstoke.co.uk
Website: www.barringtonstoke.co.uk

More books by Eric Brown!

TWOCKING

ISBN 1-842990-42-X

All of Joey's evenings were pretty much the same – hanging out and pretending to be drunk. But then Emma introduces him to twocking – taking without the owner's consent. Thrilling, dangerous, like nothing he's ever done before. Just how far will Joey go?

You can order **TWOCKING** directly from our website at
www.barringtonstoke.co.uk

More books by Eric Brown!

Firebug

ISBN 1-842991-03-5

"One match," he said. "One match is all it'd take!"

Danny has moved to a new town and things are not going well. No-one has taken an interest in him – he is bored and lonely and bullied by the cruel and violent Ross Davis. But then Danny discovers something new, something that makes him feel powerful.

But will he know where to stop?

You can order **Firebug** directly from our website at **www.barringtonstoke.co.uk**